I0788535

UNDERSTANDING THE MISUNDERSTOOD

UNDERSTANDING THE MISUNDERSTOOD

TIA BENINCASE

J Merrill Publishing, Inc., Columbus 43207
www.JMerrillPublishingInc.com

ISBN-13: 978-1-954414-02-0 (Hardback)
ISBN-13: 978-1-954414-01-3 (eBook)

Title: Understanding the Misunderstood
Author: Tia Benincase
Cover Design: Rebecacovers

CONTENTS

1

———————

CHRISTY

So like, where do I go from here? Everyone has their own fucked up life stories. You know, the kind that can be turned into a movie. Yea, a movie of my life would be great and confusing all at once.

It would be a story of a little girl that grows up wanting to be a stripper or porn star. Call me "N. Nasty" or "Icy!" I don't know why but I really hope to be a dancer someday. Not really a stripper but hell, it would have worked out still okay for me.

Let's not get off topic but a porn star because sex was my high point. Sex umm hard to say if I am the best, but needless to say, I like to feel on top.

Born on the back of the bus in a little town south of Ohio valley. My mother, Dian, and my father, Nate, named me Christy.

My mother was fifteen, a freshman at Central High School, and my dad was just about to be eighteen. He was a varsity football player team cap, and as we all know, the cool guy. How they got together beats me. I just know they ran away, got jobs, and raised me.

When I was about six years old, I overheard my parents yelling, "When the fuck were you going to tell me?" The door shut, and the next thing I know, my daddy was rushing into my room, taking me away from my mother. That night I never understood why my dad and I left. I just know he would kiss me before bed and say, "Sorry, child, you're still my babe."

As I grow up, I have slowly forgotten I even had a mother. My father put me in the best school and spots he could afford being a DEA officer. By the time I was a preteen, I had started noticing some things about my father and me.

My father was 6'1" and had smooth, light brown hair with blue eyes and pasty white skin. On the other hand, I had jet black hair that was very much nappy and a tan that all my friends wanted. My father would take me to all the black hair shops to get my hair done and buy all the clothes I liked. Not once did I see color.

My dad's best friend, Stacy, an officer who worked with my dad, would come over every now and then to play poker or watch a game. Father would call me in the room to join the fun and told me I would understand who I was one day. I never understood that man. I shook my head and laughed as kids do.

One night Stacy ask my dad, "Hey Nate? Ya think she ready?" My dad looked at me and said yea. I was confused and lost; I didn't know what was going on.

Stacy took my hand and said to me, "Little Miss, it's time you know!"

I looked at my dad, "Daddy, what's wrong? What's going on? Stacy, let my hand go!"

"Now, Nate, tell her!"

"Tell me what??? Daddy? Daddy?"

He still said nothing. He put his head down and said, "11 years ago, I met the love of my life, and she was a beautiful as you. She had smooth skin like pudding and was as white as me."

"Okay, daddy and...?"

"Listen, Christy, look at you. Now, look at Stacy!

"Okay??"

Just tell her yelled Stacy.

"I am not your father, and we found your mother dead today."

"Umm, what are you talking about, daddy? Is this some kind of game?"

When my father looked up, he was crying. "Baby, look at you. I am white, and you are not!"

"Sooo, daddy, a lot of people come out different. No one is the same skin color."

Confused about this whole white thing and not being my daddy, I run to my room, where I hid under the bed, hoping this was a dream.

Then it hit me. My mother, my mother is dead, and I didn't even know her. Father entered the room, dropped a box, then walked out. Before he shut my door, he said, "Soon and very soon, you will know who you are, my love.

I cried and cried because I was lost, and I didn't know what this means. Was he going to give me away like I have seen in the movies or what?

The only man I've known as my father was not my father, and the lady that I never known, my mother, was dead.

2

WAKE THE FUCK UP!

"Hello, Miss Christy!"

"Yea, yea, I am here. Sorry, sometimes it is hard to come back."

"It is okay, we will talk some more tomorrow. By the court order, you have to complete all required hours with me, and so far, it's been day 1 out of 10."

"I understand, Doctor Bitch."

"Excuse me? Did you say something?"

"Umm, no, doctor. Just saying, see you tomorrow."

"Oh, okay, have Ty sign your paper on the way out!"

Damn, nine days to go talking about my life. That bitch thinks I need help, all because I cut his dick almost off. Now, for some reason, instead of jail time since he did rape me, I got to report to a fucking lady that says I have suppressed childhood anger. Whelp, that's better than jail for attempted murder.

Today is a big day for me. I am turning 30 and about to become the vice president of the top-selling movie company "Ain't This Shit Grand?" Plus, a night on the town with my best friends James and his boy toy Lex. "Omg, it's going down. Hopefully, I'll find me a man tonight, someone that can rock my world and send me home wishing that I was into forever laughing out loud. Just another one of those things I don't have time for, relationship and freelance sex and all that BS. Just me and my toy topping me off tonight!"

Girl, you silly! James, you just in love with dreams.

At least my dreams got a big oops, not something that only lasts for a second until you break it. Shaking my head, "Where are we off to, my love?"

"To the hall of fame."

Sitting in the car, I found myself thinking about high school. My first boyfriend, Chris, had the sweetest voice a guy could have. I started talking to Chris in my senior year in music class. Chris was not just any old body; he was the guy everyone wanted, but I had.

My father hated him, and that made me love him. Every day we would take walks to the park and ride around in his car to show me off to his boys. I loved the attention.

One night, we took a ride down past 2nd street, where my father used to say that there was nothing but drugs and gangs over there. We pulled up to this house, and Chris said to me, "Hey CeCe, get out."

I was so damn nervous I said, "Umm, why? You know I can't be here."

"Oh, come on, love, I got you."

We walked up the stair to the door. He tapped the door softly, opened it, and an old lady with a little voice yelled, "Damn boy, it took you long enough to get your ass in the house! I have been up waiting on you. I was worried something happened to you."

"Ma, I told you I was going to be late."

"Who the girl with you?"

"This is CeCe, the young lady I was telling you about."

Chris, this is where you stay?

Yea, I wanted to tell you, but I don't want you to look at me the wrong way.

Well, come on, have a seat, tell me about you, she said.

"Ma, we need to study."

Oh, okay.

Come on, CeCe.

We got into his room; he shut the door and said, "Soo my love, what do I do now that I got you here?"

Boy stop. You know I got to be going home soon.

A few seconds later, he got a call. He jumped up, grabbed me, and ran to the car.

Man, what's up?

Nothing love sorry bad timing you can't be here.

He dropped me off at my door and didn't even say bye.

The next day in school I didn't see him. I called and called his phone but no answer. By the time week two came around, I am so pissed that I didn't notice that he was standing behind me with a card and flowers.

I was standing in the hall talking to some girl, telling her that I am so over this. By the time I turned around, he had picked me up and kissed me. We never talked about what happened the day he dropped me off. It was like it never happened. So, we started spending more and more time at his house.

On one hot summer day, my father had taken off for work early and told me he would be in. In the morning, I kissed as I always do, said love you, and shut the door.

Waiting for him to pull off, I called Chris. "Hey, baby, do you want to come over? My dad's gone for the day."

Rushing up to the bathroom, not knowing what I was doing, I took a shower. I shaved all the hair off my body that I could find, even cutting myself a few times. Then I found the shortest pair of boy shorts I have and a tight and thin tee-shirt.

By the time he got to my house, I felt like a mold. I pulled out my father's old video recorder and placed it at my bed top, and when I open the door, he just looked.

"Hi, do you want to PLAY?"

As he laid me down on the bed, I whispered, "this is my first time." He laughed and told me this is not his.

He looked up, pushed play, and started to kiss me from head to toe. Placing his lips on my clitoris and kissing it like my lips, then he put his middle finger in me slowly. I did not know what to do but lay still.

By the time he put his dick in me, I was over the fact that we were really having sex.

Our bodies intertwined like two vines that could not be parted.

Hand on my, lips on my, "Please don't stop. I need you," I cried out. "Harder, deeper, yes yes oh, fuck daddy take me."

By the time we finished, I looked at my watch and yelled, "Oh my god, you got to go! My father should be here soon!"

He jumped up, kissed me, and took off. I took my tape, placed it into the box under my bed, and showered up. By the time I got out, my father was in the kitchen making a cup of tea and asking how did I sleep?

At school the next day, it felt like everyone know what I did.

Chris came to me and said we needed to talk and that it was very important to meet him in the gym. After I was finished with my lunch, I rushed to the gym and saw him with this older girl hugged up.

"What is going on, Chris?

Umm, she and I think you should date someone on your own speed.

What?

Yea, fuck, we just fucked. I gave you me. I don't mean nothing to you?

He laughed and said, "naw, I am just not ready for all you doing. Baby, you want too much from me."

Right there, I made a promise never to fall for dick. Love is a losing game, and I have to play it head-on.

3

OUT OF CONTROL

In college, I had my fair share of men. I learned things I could do with my body that it took females my age a life to do to.

Party after party, no one could fill this empty feeling inside of me that called out for heat, passion, and love. No one could love me like I wanted or needed. Sex became a game to me.

I would tape each person like if it was for a project and they were my study. Over the years, I filled up tons of boxes under my bed that soon would need a new space. College was no longer an adventure to me; I needed new faces and bodies to enjoy.

By June of 2000, I needed money to pay for my classes. A friend said that she had a job for me, and I could make a grand a week. All I had to do was sit in a room, passing out bags.

She gave me a number and a bag; if I wanted it, call.

Classes and my need for love were getting to me. The next day, I called the number, and a lady answered. She asked me a few silly questions and told me to come in.

That night I dressed in my Sunday's best and went to this shop. I still didn't know what the hell I was doing.

I asked to speak to the owner.

"Hi, I am Jen, you can call me Miss Jay! You have no name here, and you only get cash."

"What will I be doing?"

She laughed and said, "What are you good at?"

"I don't know ! What can I say? I do a lot".

She took my hand and walked me to her office, shut the door, and said, "Take a seat."

I did as I told, still wondering what the fuck did I get myself into.

She opened her mouth and said, "I am a woman of many titles, and my job is to please my customer. This is not a hoe house; it's a funhouse. Your job is to have fun."

"Umm doing what, Miss Jay?"

"Fucking, little girl. I don't think this is for you."

I stood to my feet and walk to the door. Oh shit, this bitch is crazy, shaking my head as I went to turn the handle.

I got into the hall and stood there looking at men and women walking around happy. You could even hear yelling, the type you wonder what could feel that good.

I turned back to the door and said, "Oh lord, I am going to do it."

"Umm, I see you want to play!"

"Yea, I mean, yes, Miss Jay."

Come here, let me get a look at you.

She put me in front of her and said, "You like a rose I use to know, my favorite flower that I lost. If only you had milky white skin and hair like silk, you would be my Di... Oh, but let's get you ready."

Over the next month, I had become some doll that was about to be everyone's favorite toy. She set me up with a shit load of appointments from doctors to hair to makeup and clothes.

Miss Jay treated me differently from everybody else. She made sure I felt on top of the world; she never let me feel unloved.

When it was time for me to start working, I was well on my way to becoming a pro. I know dick like it was the back of my hand; no color, shape, or size was too much.

Shit was going good until SHE came in...

4

MY WILD CARD

It has been a year since I have been working. My tape boxes are taking up more space than I have to hide them, seeing how my bed was too small and so was my room. It was time for me to say goodbye to living at home and move into my own place, seeing how I had only a year left in school and I was already about to be 21 years old.

It was easy to hide my tapes and lifestyle from my father because he never stepped into my room after placing that box by my bed. It's been eight years since we really talked, my father had shut me out of his world, and I don't know how to speak to him anymore.

I found this place outside the city near my job and school. It was a real distance from my father's place, but it gave me my space.

My apartment was a nice-sized two-bedroom that gave me room to place every video that I have ever made. Rent was cheap, so I could set up an entertainment system worth more than anything I owned just for the days I wanted to play back my favorite moments.

Back at work, a new face. She was a pretty young girl with skin as dark as the midnight sky and as smooth as a baby's skin. To top that, her hair was so black that it was as if it was dipped in the blackest paint and so long it covered her ass.

Okay, newbie, I see you. The bitch had nothing on me still!

She was just another lost soul in this game to me until Miss Jay started giving her my love. I was in awe when the love I had was being given to the new thing.

I was not gay, nor have I ever been with a female, but Miss Jay was something new. She gave me love that I never had; she was filling up my empty spot. I had to find out what she had that I didn't, and I needed to get my love back.

See, Miss Jay owed me this love since she had stolen it from me as a child. She took my family away, and I wanted her to pay. I had been looking for her, and when I found her, she was mine.

In that box placed at my bed as a child, told me what I had to do. I read my life step by step, and I know who I was to become, my mother's, and maybe my father's, little lady.

Now that this new fun toy is in the picture. I watched her every move and even found my way to record her as if I didn't have too much on my plate as it is.

School had reached its ending point, and my job was slowly getting there, as well. Night after night, I would watch the new project. I called it "Wild Child." It had taken over my life.

I needed more time if I was going to do this right. I needed her fast.

5

WILD CHILD, YOU'RE MINE NOW!

Time was moving too slow for me, and I know if I waited anymore that it would not happen, I would lose this game. The time is so right I made my move.

She was outside alone, heading home. I stopped:

"Hey, baby doll. I know we don't talk, but I was wondering if we can go get a cup of whatever is open? I need some pointers about a client that we share."

"Oh, okay, sure! Let me call my girlfriend and tell her I'll be home later on."

"Okay, that's fine."

I waited for her to get off the phone. We then got in my car and went to a little bar.

On the way, I asked her questions about a guy we spent time with. I got her to open up.

• Step one: Make her feel like I needed her.

• Step two: I asked her about her personal life.

Knowing I already know everything she was about to tell me, I order her favorite drink over and over again. She was amazed and really got relaxed.

• Step three: get her to go home with me.

I told her how I was so alone and need some company tonight, how she was the only friend I had, and I enjoyed spending time with her. She agreed, and just like that, we were back on the move.

Once we got to my place, I took her coat off and put on some music. Funny, she said, "I love this song. It gets me so in the mood."

"In the mood for what," I asked?

"You know, in the mood."

I walked to her and stood behind her. I placed my hands on her hips and kissed her neck as soft as I watched her lover do. Then I grabbed her hair from the middle of her head, pulled her to me some more, then as she went to turn to me, I walked away.

"Sorry, I don't know what happened. I just got lost in the mood, I guess."

She walked to me and said, "it's okay. This must be your first time, huh?"

"First time what? With a female? Yea!"

"Don't be nervous. I got you."

Now let the fun begin, I said to myself. I picked her up and put her on my kitchen table. I pulled her legs apart and kissed her neck down to her breast.

As she got more into it, so did I. I placed my hand on her inner thigh and rubbed her pussy 'til she was wet. I wondered what it felt like to put my finger in her.

She yelled, "Keep going!" So I did.

I went as deep as I could go to the point that I forgot what I was doing with her. I started to enjoy this more than I should. So much that I dropped down and licked and sucked her as if she was my favorite pie and ice cream.

Next thing, we were in my bed. She had me face down and was licking and shoving her finger in me so hard... IIIII!!!

Oh shit!! I'm soo off-topic! I need to refocus on what the fuck I am doing.

The other night I went to the store and bought some rat killer, a deadly powder to anyone or anything that ate it. I had mixed it with some wipe cream that I bought, and I know she would love it.

I stopped her and put a bit on my nipples and a bit down my belly, just enough where she would make it through the night. After she finished, I got up and made her a bath, washed her up, and let her rest.

When the morning came, I tapped her to see if she was still alive, and she was, so I made a cup of juice with some of my dear rat killer and took her to breakfast at a diner that had been known for making people sick.

She begins to eat, and out of nowhere, she started coughing up blood.

I yelled, and people around rushed to the table calling 911, but as you know, she didn't make it. The diner was shut down for health code issues, and her death marked food poisoning.

It's been two months, and she was gone. I was back at number one in Miss Jay's heart and thanking God for it. Business had picked up, and I was good.

Miss Jay and I became closer, and I started feeling that empty spot again. Why was I empty when I had her? What made me hurt again? Was it the fact that I killed, or was it the fact that I let her make love to my body without my heart?

It was time to step up my game get to Miss Jay the way she got to my father when I was six.....

6

PARTY'S OVER, BACK TO THE DOCTOR

As the night ended with James and it was time to go back to reminiscing with this bitch, I thought about what would happen at the end of all this.

"Hello, doctor! Can we begin? I have a long day."

"Sure, but be for we start, how was your birthday?"

"It was okay!"

"That is good to know. You left off at this box that your father left you!"

"Oh yea, after he shut the door, I came from under the bed and opened the box. In the box were letters to mother from this guy named Timothy. He sent my mother letters every day date back before I was born. One letter I read was about how he was sorry he left her, but her dad was never going to approve of him. Also in this box were notes that were addressed to him, but all returned.

"I found pictures of me and mommy that my dad had taken. Pictures of my dad and mother in school, pictures after I was born, they looked happy! It had taken me months to read every letter. My father would explain each one to me when I got lost or did not understand something in them.

"Through the course of my letters, I found out just who Timothy was. He was a young black man from down south who moved to Ohio and lived next door to my mother .... The story went on, and I found out this is my father, and he left my mother because of my grandfather.

"I also found out that my father, Nate, knew my mother was having a child before they started dating. My father did not know that when I was five, my mother and Timothy hooked back up. Mother began doing drugs and working at a so-called bar where she slept with men for money.

"Timothy left her because of the lies and knowing she was married. My mother stated in one letter that she was heartbroken because the only men she knew did not know her, and they both would walked out on her. She said she hoped I would never be like her and that she loved us but was lost.

"Doctor? I need to stop!"

"What is wrong?"

"Why would a person that loves you hurt you? Well, do not answer that just yet!

I'll keep going now. Although this was only a year before me and my father left, it seemed longer, and a lot of shit happened. Once we were out of the picture, my mother tried to get clean and even moved home to her parents' house.

Years went on, and she was doing good. Reading her newfound journal, she kept made me feel like I was in her shoes. She went to college and did all kinds of new and what seemed to be fun things.

Mother wrote one year about a new friend she had met. This was the start of her life. She titled it in her journal. She writes about a girl named Jen. They were around the same age, but Jen lived a different life than my mother. Jen was wild, carefree, and adventurous.

Jen took my mother on as a sidekick where I go you go was Jen's favorite thing to tell my mother. Jen shared secrets with my mother, as did my mother with Jen.

As time went on, Jen promised my mother that she would never leave her like my father and Timothy did. She made sure my mother wanted for nothing. Jen and my mother became one, and nothing could come between them.

In one event, my mother tells Jen she had missed her child and wanted to see her baby.

Jen got upset and hit my mother over the head with a cast-iron pan and said to her that she had no one but her and loved no one but her. If my mother ever tried to run away, she would kill her.

Mother gave details about this event that made me angry and pissed. I had to put the journal away for a few months. It was too hard to read what happened over the next six months.

By the time I picked up the journal again, I was ready to read if my mother got away from Jen, but it was the end of the journals and letters no more to tell, and I was lost.

I asked my father how my mother died. He said she was cut ear to ear, put in an empty house with a needle hanging out her arm with a note pinned on her chest!

"Daddy, what did it say?" I asked very angrily?

It said: "To my dear Rose, with this, I send you to your maker, but with the hope that you know my love for you was deeper than you could see. I showed you with this here knife how deep it was and the pain you put on me. Rose as white as the snow, as beautiful as the land that God made you. I now let go..."

Doctor! May I go now? I cannot do this, and I really must be getting back to work.

Sure your time is up for today. Would you like to just call this day three? I see how this has upset you.

Wow, you are not that bad after all. Hey doc, what is your name?

My name is Jones!

No, your first name, if you don't mind.

Oh, it's Na'Diance. My father named me before he died.

Oh, sorry to hear that you have a unique name.

Thanks, see you soon.

7

COUNT DOWN

Days went on, and Doctor Jones and I discussed everything I thought was important for her to know about me. I danced around real shit that could lock me up, but I kept her interested in wanting to learn more about my life. I told her what she wanted to know. Even up to the event that got me here, or should I say that help me get here faster.

From her understanding, the court ordered me to see her because I was out with a few of my friends, a man pulled me into an alley and raped me. Before he could finish, I found a broken bottle and cut his dick.

Now, if anyone really paid attention to the man's medical record, his dick was cut in half years ago when he had a gender modification surgery. Also, he was gay.

It's no wonder they found blood. If I fingered myself with sharper ass nails, I would bleed too. To top that, we're both not in jail. The judge had the same name as the man. I don't know what this world is coming to, but I only had ten days to end a life and begin a new one.

My friends thought I was doing a very intensive study on Psych 101 and that helping complete my paper would somehow change the way people think.

I had become a great liar and deceiver to all who know me. My age was not true, only off by six years, and my name was true for the most part. My college studies were a 4 years degree, not if you counted the other four master's degrees before that.

My plan for the perfect murder was in the making, and everyone would help me some way or another. I was going to put all my hard work and money into this.

8
———

MISS JAY

Miss Jay had a past. At one point, she was a mother to a little girl named Na'Diance, who today would be in her late 20's or something. I hear that she is a Doctor.

Miss Jay lost her child after she had her because of drugs and some other shit she never really went into. She and I became really friendly with one another to the point I had her in my bed at night and making me breakfast in the morning. Hell, she even gave me a key to her apartment and office. She told me that I was the only one in her life she cared about and wanted to take it to the next step.

Oh, how this was working out for me. Getting her to open up about her past was as easy as it could be. She told me about her Rose who left her and the man named Nate that fathered her child then ran off with her Rose.

I know there was so much more to my mother's death than just what my father told me and the letter I read.

The time came for me to take Miss Jay out. I was lost and needed more information about my father. I needed to know why he left her and did he know about the child.

I Had to stop my dancing with the devil just until I heard his side of all this. I know this part would not be easy, but it should be interesting to find out who the hell I really am.

Dancing without music to the sounds of pain, to kill them as they did me to open doors that will set my soul free!

It was time I did a study on my father and see what he was hiding. It has been over a year, and I have not spoken to my father face to face. Oh, how I missed him so much.

Today was the day I get my answers about my father, Nate, who killed my mother and why?

Although my days with Doctor Jones were over, I still called her to see how she was and just talk.

9 781954 414020